Living in a Bubble

and other stories

by M. A. Fink

illustrations by Valen LaRae

I0520905

The story "For Want of Axial Tilt" was first published in the Fall 2014 issue of Local Nomad: An On-line Journal of Writing & Art. www.local-nomad.net

The stories "Incident at Squeaky's", "Living in a Bubble", and "Singular" were first broadcast on R. B. Wood's "The Word Count Podcast", as read by the author. This is their first time in print.

To Jean Vengua

Acknowledgements

Thanks to R. B. Wood and "The Word Count Podcast," without which several of the stories in this book may not have happened. Go give his show a listen. You might just hear me read something out loud. http://rbwood.com

Thanks as well to Sarah Pacetti. A fine illustrator herself, she introduced me to a plethora of talent when I was searching for someone to create the images you'll find inside this book. I was lucky to hire Valen LaRae; it was Sarah who helped me find her. http://sarahpacetti.blogspot.com

Which brings me to Valen! Such marvelous images. Her skill and humor were more than I could have hoped for. Read her bio at the end of this chapbook.

Living in a Bubble

Meredith's stomach growled loud enough to wake her from a dream: she had been playing tag with her PuppyPal when it made angry noises at her. This was so out-of-character for the synthepet that Meredith realized she must be dreaming; that her PuppyPal (whom she had named "Creeper") had been deactivated years ago. Waking, she opened her eyes to the Bubble.

A Vex was staring at her, not two meters away.

Meredith forced herself to stare back for as long as she could stand. Then she sat up, adjusted her topstrap so it covered her modesty (though she had no reason to believe a Vex would care), and stepped out of bed onto the cold, transparent floor.

Everything was cold, now.

She stepped into the sanitizer, pulled down her too-thin sleeping pants, and sat on the toilet. The Vex wandered her way after about thirty seconds — in no hurry, as usual, to resume staring at her. To her surprise, it then blinked its single yellow eye and floated upwards, perhaps to commune with its brethren, although if they were there she could not make them out in the green murk.

But of course they were there. They were always there, somewhere. Waiting.

She used to think it was cool to have a transparent sanitizer and a glass bedroom. Living in air-filled bubbles on the floor of this alien ocean was once the most novel, most exciting thing a young girl could imagine, and it happened to her and her family. The thought of sleeping, undressing (even, after several tantalizing months, masturbating) in a "fishbowl" made her mind reel and her heart flutter. Sure, her parents had stressed that, due to refraction, all anybody would see from outside was a curved mirror unless they were up very close…too close to be accidental, was her Mom's pointed remark…but it certainly seemed like Meredith was on scandalous display. After all, she could see a fair distance into the greenish fluids that made up the ocean on this planet, at least during the forty-odd hours of full daylight out of every hundred. At night, or even, like now, during the interminable twilight hours, it was a different story. The Bubble, as her family called the whole modular enclosure, used to flood the general area with electrochemical lights, but lately those had to be kept dark.

Finished on the toilet, she pressed the disposal button. Its usual chirp and whoosh sounded painful and slow, but it worked. Meredith figured today was the last day she could count on that.

She sanitized her hands, pulled up her pants, and left to enter the Family Room. The door groaned like an old woman until, impatient, Meredith squeezed her body through the opening and into the much larger living dome. She was in the midst of adjusting her topstrap again when she froze.

Five…no, six Vex were peering at her, their gelatinous, alien eyes almost pressed to the glass. More could just be seen hovering in the gloom

She ground her teeth, reached for what used to be her mother's shirt, and put it on without a sound. She wiped a hard fist over her watering eyes. The Vex wouldn't care if she cried, but she would.

Or maybe they did care. Who knew?

She put a plastic cup under the kitchen spigot, which rewarded her with a clear line of water so thin it made her spine shiver. The purifiers could provide an endless supply of water, but they needed power to do so.

She remembered a time, somehow, when there weren't any Vex—when she lived in a warm, well-lit Bubble with her parents, helping them with their research when she was not engrossed in her own studies.

Then, one by one, the Vex appeared. Mom in particular had been fascinated by them. Where had they come from? The surveys had no record of any animal life larger than a minnow on the entire planet, much less the Vex, each as big as the robotic Rovers they used to use for their own surveys. That is until the Vex, with a sudden and scary coordination, disabled each Rover by chewing or ripping at the power cables. It was when her father discovered they had previously destroyed the cables on their transmitter, their communication lifeline to the other remote teams, that he had dubbed them the "Vex."

Meredith drank what little had collected at the bottom of the cup. The line of water diminished until it was just a quick drip. She stared at each droplet, her arms limp, her body shivering in little quakes of gooseflesh under the thin garments. Her tongue felt like a fat, velvet slug in her mouth.

When the Vex had begun to gather at the generator, her mother volunteered to put on a softsuit and head to the next Bubble for help. The argument had been loud, but brief; there was nothing else to do. It was a long trip to make without a Rover to hold on to, but Mother was up to it. The rebreathers could last twenty hours on a charge if they had to. The nearest Bubble to theirs was an eleven hour swim away. Four hours swimming, one hour resting, no food but liters of drinking water…it could be done if one was fit.

Meredith and her father had watched in sick fascination as a single Vex broke off from the gathering to float after the disappearing figure of her mother. It was slow, too slow, but the very idea that one was in a kind of pursuit had frightened them to their cores.

With a grim intensity Meredith had never seen before, her father had cannibalized parts from the airlock repair kit, along with leftover plumbing supplies, to make two spring-loaded crossbows. For arrows he ground down optical conduits until they were sharp enough to draw blood just from their own weight against bare skin.

"Why two?" Meredith had asked, already knowing the answer.

"In case I don't make it back, either," her father had failed to say.

Thirty hours later, the main power went out. They were surviving on batteries. Night had fallen, the floodlights were at one-quarter brightness, and her father was putting on his softsuit. Crossbow and ten "arrows" strapped to his back, his last words to Meredith were about what she'd expected.

Now, a weak, greenish dawn light flowed into the gloom like honey over ice. Meredith could just barely see past the Bubble's immediate surroundings.

Taking her time, she counted forty Vex. She had twenty arrows for her bow. The dripping sound from the spigot stopped.

She entered the airlock, unpacked the one remaining softsuit and, no longer shivering, began to undress.

Singular

The first thing to hit me as I stepped through the metal door was the smell, like the time Ollie tried to off himself by sticking a smuggled hairpin into a light socket. The second thing was how clean the lab was. Spotless and smaller than I imagined—maybe as long as a bowling lane and, I don't know, twenty feet wide.

Doctor Barnale sat in a folding chair with barely enough room for his legs behind a crowded workstation. It was clear he hadn't heard me enter. A large white clock on the wall said I was exactly on time. I cleared my throat in that way I remember folks in movies do, polite-like.

"Yes?" His eyes were wide and wet behind funny, square glasses. "Who are you?"

"Uh, I'm Marcus, Doctor Barnale. We met a few weeks ago." He still looked blank. "I'm the, uh, volunteer."

His head did a strange little dance. "Oh, for Christ's sake, of course! Marcus. Good lord, man, I'm sorry. I didn't recognize you without...that is, er..."

"My ex always said orange wasn't my color."

He chuckled, but I could see his ears blaze, just like my dad's did when Mom caught him at something. "Well, it won't matter anyway," he said. "For the test, I mean."

I wasn't sure *what* he meant until a couple of seconds went by. "You mean I can't wear...I'm going to be naked?"

He shrugged. "Well, yes. Is that a problem?"

"No, sir." It didn't come out right away, but still pretty quick. I got naked for inspection twice a week; doing it one more time to ditch it all was not a problem.

"Good, that's good. It won't be for long, anyway." He plucked a few times at his nose like his glasses were bothering him. "Have you been fasting?"

"Yes, sir, twelve hours as ordered."

"Excellent." The chair scraped on the concrete floor as he stood. I must have winced or jumped or something because he gave me a new look. "You nervous?" He waved it off without waiting for an answer. "Don't be. As I said at the interview, this has been done hundreds of times on animals. It barely made them blink."

"I know, Doctor Barnale." My eyes finally found what I didn't even know they'd been searching for: two silver wire baskets maybe fifteen feet apart hanging from the ceiling like they were fancy lamps. On the floor right beneath them were round steel platters with rubber or black plastic rims.

He tapped a few things into a wide keyboard. "But...?"

"I'm sorry, sir?"

"Don't get me wrong, Marcus," he said. He was busy reading some lines of equations or whatever, but his voice didn't sound distracted at all. "If this was an established technology my bosses wouldn't have to trawl prisons for volunteers." He finally glanced at me again. "What did they promise you?"

"Time served, sir." My mouth was dry as talc.

"So you're a free man after this?"

"Yes, sir."

"I guess that explains the haircut and pressed slacks." He smiled, not mean at all.

"Yes, sir." I tried to give him a friendly smile back, but I could tell it didn't make it to my face. I felt a weird flutter in my gut.

"I swear, Marcus, this will be the easiest time served in history." He pointed a stubby finger at one of the disks. "Just yesterday a chimp named Leslie stood right there one moment, then... " He snapped his fingers, pointing to the other disk. "… right there the next moment. She's done it so many times she's bored with the whole thing." He shook his head and laughed. "In just a decade or three, everyone will think it as commonplace and mundane as a chimpanzee does now."

I bit at the next words, my forehead getting warm because I didn't want to fuck up the whole deal, but it was no good. "But is it the same monkey?"

"Ape," Doctor Barnale said automatically. "Chimps are apes. And, yes, the Leslie that arrived was identical to the Leslie that left."

"That don't mean it was the same mon… chimp," I said. I knew there was nothing I could do now but see this through.

"Ah," he said, nodding. "I see what this is about. Yes, something like this always gets brought up." He chewed at his lip for a second. His right hand still tapped in some commands, like it was trained separately for the job. "You wonder when I press the 'transmit' button if the Marcus on the disk doesn't just die and his clone replace him."

"That's exactly it," I said loudly. I tried to cool it down some, but that just made my voice shaky. "If he has all my memories, he'll think everything was…that it turned out just like you said. And not him or nobody could prove that I, that me…that I didn't just snuff it on the thing, there." I wiped at my mouth. "At the beginning."

He shrugged. "I'd go," he said. "They won't let me. But that's how sure am I of the process, Marcus. The math is ironclad: there is no possible test, in practice or even in theory, that could distinguish between the person on the first pad and the one on the second. At no time will you exist in two places at once, even for a nanosecond. Each particle's spin and charge will be precisely the same and, in quantum mechanics, that literally makes them identical." He held up a finger. "Not a 'copy'. Identical."

I stared at the rig. "You'd go," I said.

"In a heartbeat. And, someday soon, I will."

I still stared at it, as if waiting for the machine to look back.

"Marcus, son, if you've changed your mind..."

"No." The word fell out of my mouth like it was a brick. "No, sir, let's do this. Do I gotta get undressed now?"

His lips curled in a wry kind of smile. "Might as well, everything's set up. Put your clothes on that rack, there, and step up to the closest platform. It will just be half a minute."

I did what I was told. The air was really dry; my shirt crackled as I pulled it over my head. When I had everything off but my socks I just looked at them on my feet, wondering if I would recognize them the next time I saw them.

"Ready, Marcus, go on up."

I took off the socks and draped them over the plastic laundry rack. I glanced at the metal disk, sideways-like.

The next few steps were some of the toughest I'd ever made.

There was a pop.

*** *** ***

"See, Marcus? Did you feel anything at all?"

Marcus looked at the walls, his hands, then down to his bare feet. He seemed bemused, maybe relieved. "Oh, no, hardly anything. I heard a popping like chewing gum and maybe a breeze, but nothing really much at all." To Doctor Barnale's amusement Marcus wiggled his toes.

"Get dressed, Marcus. I need to ask some detailed questions. We can use the break room."

"Sure, Doctor Barnale." The nude man, his face alight like a newborn's, stepped gingerly off the platform, took a few steps and reached for his socks.

Timbuktu

Timothy was an only child,
pouty and shy, extremely mild.
He didn't know Mom,
but Dad was there
usually sitting in his chair.

Dad was always gruff and meaty;
used to travel during B.T.
(That mysterious time
Before Tim was there,
Dad loved to fly most anywhere).

Children grow up, it rarely fails.
Timmy grew to dislike the tales
Dad often told
of his trips and travails
searching for impossible grails.

Tim studied math, then real estate,
anything 'cept what he'd come to hate:
Dad's burning passion
(geography)
distracted the man from Timothy.

Dad gave his son a parting gift
hoping perhaps to seal the rift:
a cheaply framed shot
of father and son
when Dad was thirty and Timothy, one.

Several months later, after a day
of spinning some deals, earning his pay,
Tim finally looked
(really studied the thing)
Dad in the photo was wearing a ring.

"Dad never married," Timothy said
quite overcome with gathering dread.
"He barely knew Mom,
or so it's been said...
Dad always claimed that Mother was dead."

He pried the picture from its glue
surprised to see it'd been torn in two.
A boy and his dad
were standing so proud...
"Who isn't there?" Tim said aloud.

Later that night, more puzzled than mad,
Timothy drove across town to see Dad.
He knocked on the door
it was open a crack
there was his father, flat on his back.

The cops, when they came, said he'd been dead
ten or twelve hours. They finally spread
the standard white sheet
just before dawn.
"Anything moved or possibly gone?"

Tim looked around, still in some shock:
the safe, the guns, the mantelpiece clock;
pinned to the wall
behind his Dad's ties
Timothy found a baffling prize.

There it was, the other half
of Tim's perplexing photograph
and who was all smiles
looking tan and slim
a woman holding... ANOTHER Tim?

"I must be dreaming," Timothy cried.
He flipped the shot to the other side.
Handwritten on back
in ink of dark blue
was only one word: "Timbuktu".

It took some work and careful hoarding
but four months later Tim was boarding
a big cargo ship
(Liberian flags)
sharing a room with boxes and bags.

Post-Monrovia, things were hazy.
Tim couldn't tell sane from crazy:
loud diesel trucks
blistering heat
bubbling stews of mystery meat.

Caravans clustered 'round smoking fires;
roads never meant for rubber tires.
Northward he trekked
and a bit east
Often by bus, occasionally beast.

Sunburned, bloodied, once almost shot,
Tim discovered new meanings of "hot".
Sandstorms sounded
like dragons hissing.
Who would notice if he went missing?

He waited out a scouring squall
sheltered by an ancient wall
when who from dust
their heads all curls
should then appear: six staring girls!

He looked at them and they at Tim,
the smallest pointed right at him.
"Puck!" she shouted
if right he heard her
(the wind was screaming bloody murder).

Then as one right off they flew
leaving Tim to wonder what to
do now — follow them?
He left the shade
and hurried to the tracks they made.

He found himself in quite a maze
of ochre walls and alleyways.
He lost the tracks
(the light was dim).
Then someone on his left said "Tim?"

Stopping short of a heart attack
Tim turned 'round and there in back
was a man who said
as if on cue
"Welcome back to Timbuktu."

Darker, sure, with a wider grin,
but he was Tim's identical twin.
"Come on in, man,
don't stand there stuck!
Have some tea. My name is Buck."

When Buck handed Tim his tea with cream
Tim figured life had to be a dream.
They talked through the night;
a great deal was said.
Then Mom arrived with amaranth bread.

Life was strange, but Tim, he stayed.
From such endings is the future made.
Under desert sun
giving fate its due
so flourished Tim. Buck, too.

Card of the Day

I've been going to this great coffee house I found a few weeks ago. I say "great," because I'm so used to thinking of it that way, but now, you know, I wonder.

I mean, the staff are really friendly, don't get me wrong. There is Gus, this crazy Indian dude with a grin you can almost hear. He talks to you like he's known you since kindergarten no matter who you are, which is actually pretty weird, but cool. Then there is Sunny, a red-headed gal almost as tall as I am. She does this amazing cappuccino foam art. Like, one time I got a cup with a pentagram floating on top, including a few astrological symbols. How she got those angles so exact I haven't a clue. Occasionally you see Belinda (I think that is her name) who is there mostly in the mornings, but she's like this incredible earth-mother type that makes the whole place smell like cloves when she's around. She has this...I don't know, way of looking at me that gives me such a hard...uh, thrill.

Russell is the manager. He has these wild facial tattoos that make his already piercing eyes into twin laser cannons, but he's always quick with a kind word or shockingly perceptive quip. For instance, my third time visiting, when I was really starting to fall in love with the place, he's handing me this espresso or whatever and comments on how cruel heartbreak can be when it's the other person that's changed. I was so flustered I couldn't form even a "thanks for the coffee," because that was just what was weighing on me at the time.

The café itself is its own character, of course, what with the weird local art hanging too high on those black and electric blue walls and the very soft music coming in through speakers I still haven't found.

But the coolest thing, maybe, was this little shelf with a blackboard underneath it. The board said "Today's Tarot Card Is:" and then someone would write in chalk whatever the card was that perched on the shelf above it. The first day I was there it was "The Six of Swords" and then, below that, "Bathroom Needs No Token, Today Only!" The second time it said "Wheel of Fortune" and "Spin for Free Coffee!" and there was a little clicker wheel next to the register. God, I thought that was so neat.

Eventually you get used to everything, I guess, so after coming here almost every weekday I barely notice the specials and I kind of stopped looking at the artwork, you know, like happens after a while anywhere. I just walk in, see who's at the tables and who's behind the counter today, get in line if there is one and order my usual (dry nonfat latté), not even any foam to make pretty.

So I did that today: I'm sitting down with the local weekly rag and a hot cup, just sipping away, already thinking about my second order, when I see Sunny looking off in the distance, like it is her turn today to have the broken heart. And that makes me look at the other staff. I see Russell kind of leaning on the counter, a red and white box I'm not familiar with sitting opened next to the coffee machine, like something you'd find under the kitchen sink...and he's pretty gloomy, too, but in a "oh well that's life, isn't it" sort of way. Then I notice Gus, by the doors, which is unusual not least of which because most days there are only two people working at any one time, but also because he's flipping the "Open" sign to the other side and maybe locking the doors. It's kind of hard to tell from here.

All this makes me take a new look at the place, wondering what has changed, and that's when I see the blackboard. Like usual someone scribbled today's card there and, sure enough, there it is on the little shelf, white horse and sickle and all, and I look down at my coffee and I think, "I was wondering what that taste was."

So, yeah.

At least they got great Wi-Fi service, you know?

Incident at Squeaky's

Manny ignored the subtle coughs of passersby as he took one last drag off his cigarette. The rain was just letting up, which was a fine thing as he had truly developed a thirst. He stepped out from under a tattered awning, flicking the filter like a pro into a soggy trash barrel. He squinted at the bank's digital clock across the street.

Well past time for a drink.

The air was that ripe mixture of fresh water and rotting garbage that he'd come to love in his decades here. The streets buzzed with the hydrophobes now crowding the sidewalks and one-way streets. The last effort of a sinking sun finally allowed a couple of golden beams through the cloud cover, landing like a Hollywood cue onto the sign of Manny's favorite watering hole: "Squeaky's", announced in flouncy red script. The wide-eyed mascot barely avoided a cease-and-desist letter from Disney as it grinned from under enormous round ears. Manny already knew who'd be there and who probably stayed home because of the rain. For Manny, though, "Squeaky's" was home.

He only just registered someone running behind him when he was shoved hard onto a bus stop bench. His own bulk kept him upright enough to spit a curse at the teen going flat-out down the sidewalk. Then a police officer leaped past Manny and after the boy. An olive drab SUV pulled to a stop at the intersection, blocking the runner from a quick escape. The teen whirled to see the officer pumping after him. Eyes as wide as the mascot leering above him, he pulled a small revolver from his jean jacket and fired.

Once. Twice.

The first shot sizzled by Manny's right ear, so close he could hear a nasty, shrill warble. The second hit the officer. A head jerked back with a dull pop. A man screamed.

The officer lay backward on the sidewalk, legs twitching like a car-crushed snake. The gunman was nowhere to be seen.

A grey-haired woman shouted for someone to call 911, but Manny saw so many phones out she needn't have bothered. His eyes were pulled back to the still shaking body of the police officer: hot blood steamed on the damp concrete, thickening the air. Manny felt his stomach pitch when he saw where the bullet had bitten the officer's face, as if a small, terrible animal had ripped a chunk away with its bare teeth.

Manny lurched to the heavy windowless door of the bar, pulled and fell inside.

"Manny?" said someone over the music gunning as always from the CD jukebox.

"Don't nobody help me up or nothin'," said Manny, apparently to himself. He huffed to his feet and blinked in the dim light. The air was its typical mess of mildew, beer, and artificial pine. Joanna was at her station behind the bar, the only woman in the place since Mama Zuzu died. The tables all stood empty; Manny could count on one hand the number of times some lost tourist chose to sit at one. All the regulars occupied the long bar, chatting and watching the television mime the sports. Patsy Cline was wailing from the juke so loud Manny could feel her in his sinuses.

Donald clapped him on the back when he made it to his usual barstool. "Looks like you got the day started without us, Manny!" He haw-hawed in the way he always did when he thinks he's made a funny. He winked and squeezed Manny's arm.

"A cop got shot outside," said Manny. He raised two fingers to Joanna to order his usual. "But I can see how no one might notice."

"A cop got what?" asked Pikey from way down the bar. His real name was Jacob Pike, but he had a sore spot about being called Jake or Jacob. "Thas' my old man's name," he said once in a monotone. Nobody had brought it up again.

"What'll it be today?" asked the bartender.

Manny frowned. "I gave you the 'Dos Equis' sign, Jo... oh!" The woman on the other side of the bar had the same shoulder-brushing hair and pale skin as Joanna, but now Manny could see it was another person entirely. She stood three or four inches shorter than Joanna for starters. She was younger, too, by ten years. "I'm sorry, I just assumed you..."

Donald interrupted. "That's Mindy."

"Minda," corrected the bartender. "Joanna's off seeing her son in Florida. I'll get you your beer."

"Uh, thanks," said Manny. He looked at Donald. "I didn't know Jo even had a son."

"I hope SHE did! Haw haw haw!" Donald mopped his forehead with an already damp napkin. "You okay there, Manny? Your hands are shakin'."

Manny looked down at his hands. His fingers were doing a queer little dance. "Yeah, well, just before I got in..."

Pikey was shouting across the bar. "You said a cop was what now? Outside?"

Donald shouted back. "Mind your own business, old man!"

Manny was shocked. "Don, what the hell? You pissed at Pikey for something?"

Donald gave him a funny look. "Pikey? You think that looks like Pikey? Pike hasn't been here in days, son, you know that."

A weird tremor scuttled sideways through Manny's breast as he peered across the bar. The man looked a lot like Pikey: same white scruff of beard, same wrinkled forehead...hell, even the same dented leather hat, more or less. But this guy had long, piano-player's fingers; dark circles pushed into eyes nowhere near as expressive or lively as Pike's. And the real Pikey would have been too surprised by Donald to be flipping both of them off like that.

"Shit." Manny squinted through a haze at the others at the bar. Instead of Lou there was a gentleman wearing practically the same tweed jacket. The squat Armenian that everybody just called "Sig" rather than tackle his real name turned out to be someone else, too. Manny had no idea who.

"You look terrible," said Donald.

Manny's eyes burned. Yet another Patsy Cline song started on the vivid yellow juke across the room, her usually clear, well-modulated voice warbling like a melted record, except he knew CDs didn't do that. A bottle of something appeared on the bar. He couldn't tell what. Manny felt a horrible tremor start in his thighs and he stared over at his friend. "What the... what the hell is happening, Don?"

"Sorry, son, can't help you there," said the stranger.

Manny opened his eyes one last time to see a circle of people he didn't know stand over him, taking photos with their phones as the warm mist rose into the last rays of the sun.

The primitive, metallic *snipznip* of an antique pair of scissors impelled Camové to crawl over on all eights to see what Matthew was up to. "She" (for that's how he experienced her) stared unblinking as he cut complex random patterns in the folds of white synthetic tissue.

Matthew suppressed a smile, but kept his focus to his task. Camové would ask in her own time. While she watched, intent as a serpent from the Old Days, the only other sound was the ever present nothing of the station's life support system.

"What are you doing?" Her voice was like sawtooth velvet.

Matthew spared a glance at her. She had no face — her kind rarely did — but she had become canny in her posing and manipulation of the smirk he had drawn on her sensory shell months ago. The simple, ironic line reclined beneath the twin green photoreceptors halfway up her glossy, bean-like carapace.

"Wait and see," he said, returning to his task. "It's almost finished."

She approached until Matthew felt his bed sink under her weight. It was unusual for her to come so close to him. He wished she would do so more often. He wished…

In no time, he set the steel scissors down and unfolded the now intricate tissue, bits of scrap fluttering down into his lap. A design with six-fold symmetry blossomed between his clean, lean hands.

Camové watched it for a second, then looked into Matthew's eyes and tilted into an artful interrogative.

"It's a snowflake," he said.

She remained unmoving.

He licked his lips. "A fake one, obviously. An oversized representation."

She seemed to consider that. "An artistic interpretation of an atmospheric water crystal."

"Sounds pretty good," he said. He raised the cut-out and turned until they looked at each other through it.

"Why?"

"I knew you would ask that." He shrugged and released his paper creation to flutter and refold in half upon the bed while he made a show of dusting the waste bits off his legs, scattering them about the floor. Camové chose not to follow as Matthew walked the short distance to his cabin's only window. He watched the stars wheel as the station turned about its axis. "I've never been to Earth."

"I thought you were born there?" said Camové.

"Not...not the New Earth Space Complex. I meant Old Earth." He struggled with the words. "The original Earth."

Camové tucked her tentacles underneath her, a model of patience.

Matthew saw this in the window's reflection and sighed. "I think you sense a story coming on," he said. "Well, there isn't one. Not this time." Bare feet scuffed an uneasy staccato. He studied his toes. "I mean, how can you miss something you never had? You'd have to go back a thousand years before you found any of my ancestors on that planet."

"Did it snow on Old Earth?"

The question drifted in the warm, close station air.

"Yes." He leaned against the window. "In most places, anyway, sometimes...during the winter."

"I don't understand that term, Matthew."

He turned around, surprised. "You knew what a snowflake was, but you don't understand 'winter?'"

"Only as an abstraction. I recognize the word from some of the music you play when you are working on the transmitter."

He cocked his head. "Music?"

"Yes...Tori Amos, Simon and Garfield..."

"Funkel," he said, grinning. "Simon and Garfunkel. I thought your kind couldn't really 'hear' music."

Two of her forward tentacles performed a complex shimmy. "I enjoy the lyrics."

He shook his head. "To think you've been listening all this time...well, my friend, classical music like that comes from Old Earth. And 'winter' was a season."

"Like salt or pepper."

"Yes. No. Homonym."

She made a motion that Matthew knew to mean *I understand.* "A climatological variation caused by axial tilt."

He snapped his fingers. "You got it."

"You miss the variations your ancestors must have experienced."

He nodded. "I suppose I do."

"Variations absent on space stations."

"Exactly."

There was the briefest of pauses. Then, in that almost feminine voice of hers, Camové said "You fear that, since the recombinant plague that forced your species into sterile environments a millennia ago, humans survived only to lose themselves in detachment from your natural order."

Matthew stared at her.

Another pause. "You are scared this is happening to you," she said, unblinking green eyes meeting his.

His thin, pale body sagged backward against the window.

"Yes."

Outside, in the unknowable cold, the stars blew in drifts across the black sky.

About the Author

M. A. Fink is the author of The Found Diary of Avery Alexander Myer, an ontological mystery novel illustrated by surrealist Gromyko Semper and published by Tornado Skin Press. He's had some poetry and short fiction published here and there, including in The Chained Hay(na)ku Anthology, published by Meritage Press; and in "Point Lobos Magazine," published by the Point Lobos Foundation. He also played the only character to survive a slasher flick called "The Wooden Gate," but good luck finding that.

About the Illustrator

Valen LaRae is a freelance artist living in Oklahoma. Art is a big part of her life both as work and a hobby. She's heavily influenced by cartoons and animations and being able to express the emotion of the moment in one image. She pursued a degree in Sequential Art at Savannah College of Art and Design and graduated with her B.F.A in 2013.

You can follow her work on Twitter and Tumblr @ValenLaRae.

www.ingramcontent.com/pod-product-compliance
Lightning Source LLC
Chambersburg PA
CBHW070654130626
46555CB00006B/2871